The Christmas Spirit

Steve Harrington

The Christmas Spirit
By Steve Harrington
Illustrated by Jim Benton

Maritime Press
P.O. Box 759
St. Ignace, MI 49781

0-9624629-1-8

Steve Harrington lives in northern Michigan. He enjoys scuba diving, walking beaches, and being a father. He tries to stay out of ditches in the winter and <u>always</u> goes home for Christmas.

For

My mother, Nina, who
showed me how to find
Christmas magic all year
long. Also for my sons,
Jason and Sam, because their
support makes nearly any-
thing possible.

The drive from Chicago seemed to get longer each time. Snow replaced a cold rain and the windshield wipers became sweeping icicles. Darkness came much too early and made driving more difficult.

There were blizzard warnings and I slipped out of work early to keep ahead of the storm. But it was one of those blizzards from the north that often herald the real winter season. The snow gradually increased and wind nudged the compact car with each gust.

This was Christmas snow. It was snow to guarantee a white Christmas tomorrow. It was snow that filled the hearts of young children in cozy homes where yellow lights shone through the storm and darkness. But it threatened me. The snow threatened to push my small car off the highway and into a ditch and keep me from home. Yes, this was Christmas snow, but I didn't have time to think about that. I had to go home.

Home was a country farmhouse outside a small town called Duncan. Home was as perfect as a postcard picture and as a child I was spoiled by Christmas carols, a large family, mountains of holiday food, and the joy of a spirit that grabbed my soul each season. But things change and souls slip away.

The highway road crews were out pushing snow off the highway with orange trucks with bright yellow beacons. The wind blew the snow right back again and it wouldn't be long before the crews gave up for the night. No one could blame the drivers. They, too, had fami-

lies who would be happy for the snow that sent them home on Christmas Eve.

I lifted my foot on the accelerator to ease the car back into the right lane after passing the slow orange road block. I was going to be late and I cursed. This was the one time of the year when everyone was expected to be home. My sister and her husband were late one year and the folks were sick with worry. I didn't want to put them through that.

Ahead of the truck, the highway became two trenches of packed snow on slippery concrete. The wind occasionally hid the trenches with blowing snow. It would not be more than an hour before drifts would cover the trenches and I would have to consider stopping for the night. Except for the snow plow trucks, the road was my own.

It was only a few miles to the Duncan exit, though. From there, it was only ten miles to the farm, but those were all country roads. If I had to stop anywhere for the night, it would have to be in Duncan. But those thoughts were put away. The radio station faded and I turned it off. It was one less little green light to keep me company.

Duncan was little more than a gas station in a wide spot in the road. There was a motel but there wasn't enough business to keep the sign lighted except during deer hunting season and when it snowed like this. There weren't any other accommodations around for miles and stranded motorists didn't have any choice but to stay at Rest-a-Way Motel.

It had been nearly a year since I had last seen Duncan. Writing dog food ads for radio and television kept me busy. Of course, I told my brother and sisters I was a hot-shot advertising executive, but Pop knew I was struggling each day with adjectives to describe dogs excited about soybean kibbles. To him, I was always Nick. Always the insecure little kid who hid tears and fears with a quick joke.

But Chicago was a far cry from Duncan. The big city was an adventure and a place to learn and grow. There was live theater, night clubs, films, galleries, major league baseball games, and a life many in Duncan only experience through magazines.

Chicago was the place to live for adventure and my new life left little time for Duncan and family. Each year I made the drive less often and my stays were shorter. Now, Christmas was my only trip back for the year. A day in the country and I would head back to the city. No sense in staying too long, there were simply too many matters demanding my attention in Chicago.

A yellow glow pierced the darkness between snowy gusts. A cluster of homes near the interchange threw dull light against the low clouds. It was a meager beacon that stirred wonder about living in such a remote area. But rural boredom, "country living" they called it, seemed to fit some people well.

Pop came to Chicago to see me and a ball game one weekend. It was a polite visit but he didn't stay long and he seemed anxious to get back to Duncan. He complained that he couldn't leave the farm for long. The farm, yeah, always the farm.

The fields around Duncan were carved from rolling woodland. Through decades of effort, the hardwoods were cut to yield only enough cropland for hay and oats. Most farmers had given up on the sandy soil but Pop was stubborn. It was Mother's small bakery and hungry motorists who found the Duncan exit that kept the family solvent.

The car fought to make its own snowy trenches as it sputtered and spun up an exit ramp. Duncan was lonely despite the cluster of dwellings. Families were huddled around fireplaces and food celebrating the season and the joy of each other. A feeling of envy for them crept over me because ten miles was a very long way. It had been a long time since it seemed important enough to come home again. Already the Chicago highways seemed to be calling me back.

The call may have been compelling but for the neon of the Duncan gas station. It was a

welcome friend on a lonely night. When I first got my license, I counted change at the pumps hoping to find enough for gas to make it home.

A convenience store replaced the service bays. It was a sign of progress. Less personal, it is easier to make money selling potato chips, pop, and beer than fixing the few radiator hoses and fan belts that found their way to the station.

A clumsy teenager reported that few cars had passed. He expected the roads to be drifted shut until morning. But since it would be Christmas morning he thought it might be at least several days before the back roads were plowed. The road crews were probably reluctant to leave their families for a truck and the promise of a long, cold journey bucking heavy snowdrifts.

I shuddered and swore as the car door slammed. These were days when I had little patience for the sentimentality of others. These were days when I had little patience for inconvenience. These were days I had little patience.

The car was only a half-mile from Duncan when the blizzard erased its glow from the mirror. Drifts were quickly building and the bottom of the car hit the white cushion as I turned off the country road and onto a little-used gravel road I once walked to town. Chicago was far behind me but for a moment I considered turning back. The gravel road was barely perceptible but I kept on for the family. No one had ever missed Christmas with the family. Still, this was the first time Chicago seemed like a better place to be for the holiday.

The folks had sold most of their land to neighboring farmers and to a hunting club that fancied deer antlers. But the folks kept the large old home. It was hard to heat the two, almost three-story farmhouse. A woodstove and fireplace consumed armloads of hardwood and kept the first floor warm.

The upstairs bedrooms were usually closed off in order to conserve heat. Tonight, even with the blizzard, the whole house would be opened up to accommodate the family. Mother probably spent a week cleaning and getting the house ready to welcome the family back. All night the old oil burner in the basement would groan to heave warm air throughout the house. The oil burner was an extra source of warmth generally reserved only for the coldest winter evenings or when the whole house was opened to welcome the family.

My brother, two sisters, and their families were probably eating dinner and doing their best to keep the conversation from wondering where I had strayed. Worry has a way of eating at the folks. No one would really feel comfortable until everyone was there, especially tonight.

Even with the kids all grown, and except for me, with families of their own, Pop and Mother acted like we were still young and had just left on an extended visit from home.

The gravel road to the farmhouse is a winding drive through woods and across fields. Road builders were loggers of a hundred years ago who did their best to avoid the swamps.

The car hit drifts and floated on the snow momentarily. The wind collected snow across the fields and dumped it in the road where it threatened to stop me for the night. But I was close now. These were the fields and forests I hunted and hiked as a child. It seemed so long ago yet so fresh. These were the places that I left for adventure. But even these places were changing as trees found the sandy soil to their liking and marched, year by year, into the fields. How long would it be before the fields were left to woodland?

It was only a few miles to the farmhouse and I could almost taste the leftovers of a turkey dinner.

Suddenly, the car slipped on a snowdrift. It jerked as it wandered off the road and into a ditch. It was wedged with snow supporting the frame and prevented the tires from finding anything solid. The tires screamed and the car shuddered as it settled in for the night.

I turned off the engine and lights and sat staring at the white shower. In the rearview mirror there were silhouettes of Christmas presents. The wind nudged the car with gusts and my breath began to fog the windows. The fog turned to ice and it was time to make a decision.

The farmhouse was only two miles away but those were difficult miles through snow drifts. Dress slacks and a trench coat were fine for the city but they offered little protection against the wind and snow. It would be a difficult trek on foot.

The other option was to stay put. The car could be started occasionally for warmth but it would be a long night.

For a moment the warmth of my Chicago apartment haunted me. I wondered aloud why I left the city. I wondered why I had not simply called and told the folks I could not make it. I would be warm and safe instead of in the middle of cold wilderness. For a moment I thought I understood why I moved away and wondered if I would ever return again—for any reason.

The minutes collected on my watch until the walk home seemed the most reasonable choice. I made the decision to walk. The Christmas presents in the mirror nodded with the gusts that nudged the car. Tomorrow, we could take Johnny Pop and retrieve them before the little ones were awake.

Johnny Pop was my father's favorite possession. Not even a new pickup truck could measure up to Johnny Pop. It was an old John Deere tractor he had christened by taking the first name of the brand and the sound it made working the soil or pulling a load. Miles away you could tell it was on the way. The muffler had fallen off long ago. The rhythm of the two-cylinder engine was unmistakable.

My father kept Johnny Pop even though he quit farming years ago. I was glad he did. Tomorrow morning, it would get us to the car and pull it out of the ditch.

That was for tomorrow. Already I was ahead in my thinking. For now, this minute, the two miles home in knee-deep snow had to be conquered. A bold gust of wind rocked the car as I made a mental inventory of my meager resources. No gloves, no hat, a scarf, top coat, dress slacks. No boots. Leather dress shoes were sure to slip on the snow. Why had I been in such a hurry to leave from the office? Why had I not thrown a pair of boots in the car? Too late.

"Two miles," I muttered to myself staring out the window. Then I remembered a game trail that ran along the ridge. Suddenly it came back to me. I could trim at least a half-mile by following that game trail.

A dozen autumns before I was huddled behind a stump along that very trail. I was nearly asleep in the afternoon sun when a small buck startled me awake. I remembered how carefully—and slowly—I moved my rifle. It was my first buck. And it was on this very trail. The familiarity filled me with new confidence.

As I closed the car door I became aware of the stinging cold that had come with the snow.

The aroma of hot rubber lingered as I stood near the back tire. The temperature was probably in the teens and with the wind blowing it felt purely arctic. I pulled my collar up, tucked the scarf around my neck, and started into the forest. I hoped the trees would offer a reprieve from the wind and hurried my step to keep warm.

The snow in the forest was just as deep as it was on the road, but there were not the drifts to wrestle. The wind was only slightly reduced and it cut through my slacks as though it met no resistance. I remembered hunting in the red wool pants Pop had given me. I wore them the day I shot the deer. Those wool pants kept the fiercest winds out but collected burrs. They weren't much to look at but they would have beat the most flashy dress slacks.

Snow was packed into the tops of my shoes, that slid like miniature skis. I ran my fingers along the upper edge of the shoes and I realized that my fingers were already numb. Just a few paces into the woods they barely felt the fluffy cold.

I quickened my pace to a slow jog and pulled my collar up again for what little protection it provided against the bite of the northwest wind. As a high school track runner I had run miles for conditioning. This night, even a hundred yards seemed like a marathon. My lungs ached for oxygen as they heaved in my chest. I leaned against a large oak tree for some respite.

The farmhouse was still a little more than a half mile away and I searched my soul for the endurance of youth. It was then, leaning against the oak, that I recognized the power of the storm. Finally, perhaps too late, I could see how the snow and wind conspired to rob me of energy.

The foot steps filled with snow nearly as quickly as they were made and I knew it was unlikely I would be able to make it back to the car—even if it could be found. My only way out was ahead. Then, in that terrible darkness, fear found a home in me.

What if I had mistaken the trail for another? What if the farmhouse was further than I thought? What if I passed out from the cold before I made it home?

It was that last fear that consumed me. I had read about people, hunters mostly, who got lost and died of exposure. Those who survived such ordeals told of confusion, numbness, and finally apathy. At the very last they did not care if they were rescued from the cold.

I buttoned the top of my flimsy overcoat, thrust hands into the pockets and slid from the oak into the storm. I cursed my poor judgment and my luck. But mostly I cursed the storm. My words began as a mutter and became a conversation with the storm.

"Blow and snow! Blow and snow!" I shouted. The cold was taking its toll on my mind. I wondered aloud how long it would be before . . . I put the thought out of my head.

My hands were jammed into the coat pockets and I wished they had found matches.

I doubted that I could start a fire anyway, but the thought of warm flames distracted me for a few seconds.

The leather soles slipped more often and I felt myself becoming more clumsy. I was more stumbling than walking and the fear came upon me once more. I shook it off with the thought of the warm farmhouse.

The thought of the warmth of the farm drove me forward as I drew my legs up from the snow like a work horse. The fireplace made the family room a cozy, comfortable place for everyone to gather near the Christmas tree. The presents would be neatly stacked and prettily wrapped. Mother loved Christmas most of all. She lived for it. Her family would be together and happy. And Pop loved whatever Mother loved.

Those thoughts gave me strength but my legs were getting numb from the cold brought by the wind. The limbs of the tall oaks above clattered against one another in a clumsy dance.

I clenched my fists inside the overcoat pockets but couldn't feel my fingers any more. They were victims of the storm and my reckless venture.

A log concealed by the snow thrust me to the ground. My hands still in my pockets, I managed to roll onto my back as I lay in the snow gasping for air.

The branches clattered even louder and dead, dry leaves on their twigs rattled their laughter. The wind was barely noticeable near the ground but I could hear it whining in the trees. Numbness in my legs made me doubt I could stand.

The fear of losing to the cold was slipping away as I found an odd peacefulness laying in the snow. I remembered sliding on Walker's Hill with our sleds. We waxed and smoothed the steel runners and raced to the bottom. The wind teased our faces all the way. At the bottom we rolled off the sleds and headed back up the hill for another run.

One time I rolled off the sled but didn't get up right away. I watched the clouds, like angel's hair, flowing across the blue sky. They were quiet, graceful sliders. It was peaceful. It was an odd quiet and I could feel the snow melting against my back. If I didn't get up right away the paralyzing cold would complete its work. I took my hands out of the pockets and pushed them against the snow to lift myself. I almost fell again because I could not feel my hands. "The cold," I told myself. "The cold will not win tonight!"

But I could only stagger to the next oak tree. I leaned again and began to think about what the family would do if I didn't make it to the farmhouse. The folks would probably think I didn't try to make it through the storm. The next morning though, they would find the car. I could see tears flood my mother's tired eyes but I could not move from the tree.

A pressure in my throat was choked back and I swallowed hard. I thought about my brother. That day sliding at Walker's Hill, he saw me laying in the snow and shouted. I didn't hear him at first and when he shouted again there was a panic in his voice. It was a tone that told of concern, as though I might have been injured.

The voice came back to me and faded. I watched clouds race across the sky sliding on unseen runners.

First my legs started, and then my whole body shivered. I couldn't control the shaking. "The cold," I told myself again, but I could not move from the tree.

The wind began to sing in the trees. It was a low, mournful song, like one I had not heard before. It was a melody harmonized by a groan I could hear inside the tree I leaned against. The trees hurt from the cold, too, I thought. The song was oddly peaceful and reminded me of laying in the snow again.

My eyes focused on the snow beneath my feet. My legs had become useless stumps and I leaned hard against the tree for support.

The taste of Mother's hot chocolate came to me. It wasn't the hot chocolate made from a powder that looked like brown water. She used whole milk and sweetened cocoa. Marshmallows melted quickly into a sweet foam on top. Mother was always sure to have it ready when we came back from sliding. I longed for a tasty mug and the warmth it promised!

Fatigue gripped me and I closed my eyes. "Soon," I thought, "soon the cold would complete its work. Soon, I would fall asleep leaning against the tree."

Suddenly, an aroma slapped me awake. It was familiar—wood burning. The farmhouse was closer than I thought! Through the trees I could see the flicker of a small light. Not the bright, brilliant light of an electric bulb, but the dull yellow of a fire. Staggering at first, then into a clumsy run, I rushed to the flicker.

Without hesitation, without looking around, without considering anything more than the warmth, I knelt at the blaze and almost stumbled into it. The flames whipped my face as I leaned close. The warmth was not quickly felt but it soon came. A dull ache grew in my fingers.

I rubbed my hands together near the fire trying to wipe away the cold and pain as they thawed. With my hands silhouetted against the fire I looked up and from across the fire gazed upon my host.

At once I recognized him as an Indian, although I had not seen any Indians such as this. He was a man of many years. His face was wrinkled and was partly hidden by strands of his long white hair. I shuddered, perhaps from the cold or perhaps from his gaze that seemed to probe my soul. It made me uncomfortable and I looked away for a moment.

So compelling an apparition was he that my eyes eventually became fixed upon him. He did not speak nor appear that he was about to do so. His eyes were dark and wise as though they had seen all the world. They pierced my body as though he were examining my most personal thoughts and I trembled again.

Among the chiseled, rock features of the Indian's face, his eyes focused on mine, like a predator judging its prey before the kill. His silence made me uncomfortable but I did not speak. The Indian's face seemed to speak for him and my shivering body for me.

The warmth slowly penetrated my fingers, hands, arms, and legs. I could feel the wetness of my slacks against my legs. The pulsing pain in my fingers eased and I could hold them closer to the fire. My host sat silently focused on my eyes.

Air came to my lungs more easily now and I wondered about the Indian. There were no reservations nearby. This man wore stained leather and fur garments.

And his stare—I wondered what it meant. I wondered if he knew what I was thinking. I wondered if he felt my fear.

I wanted to ask the old man how he happened to be in those woods. I wanted to ask him how he started the fire in the blizzard. And I wanted to know why he sat so silently.

Then, it was then that I knew, this Indian whose eyes pierced my very being was somehow part of me. Somehow I knew he had been watching me for a long time. It was a presence impossible to explain but nonetheless real. It made me shiver because it was as if I had been stripped of all I held dear, and I edged closer to the fire to avoid his penetrating stare.

It was his gaze that was most disturbing. His dark eyes saw something in me—perhaps everything. What did he see? Could anything, any part of me, hide from his gaze?

I rubbed my hands together and glanced at the Indian's feet. He was a small man, even wrapped in a thick fur hide. There was a leather pouch at his side. It was a worn, brown sack that bulged slightly at the bottom. It was tied with narrow leather strips at the top. I wondered about its contents only for a moment. The warmth of the fire was beginning to overcome the shivering and drew my attention away from my host.

I worked my legs and stood over the fire. Warm blood rushed to my toes as I studied the old man again. As I stood he dropped his gaze into the fire. Not to the fire but into the fire. It was as if his eyes were capable of piercing the flames as they had pierced me.

I turned so the fire could warm my back and I looked straight up. I suddenly became aware that the wind had calmed and stars were twinkling. The trees no longer moaned and branches had ceased their clumsy dance. It was quiet, silent except for the muffled crackling of burning wood.

My mind paused to wonder how the wind could cease so quickly and how clouds could disappear so completely. I also wondered how the old Indian had come to be on that trail that raw night. For a moment I thought I was about to ask the old man, but his gaze was too intense upon the flames and I thought better of it.

The flames had done their work and I was warm again. More than that, I felt a new energy and new sense of urgency. Home. The only thing that mattered now was getting home.

I gathered my clothing around me and prepared to hike the last half-mile to the farm-house. As I stepped I realized that we all have fears of some sort. On the ridge I faced my fears. Had it not been for the Indian I would have perished.

With the wind calmed I was certain I could make it. I stepped from the fire and into the coolness. My mysterious host did not return my gaze or half-hearted wave. I turned and began again the trek home.

Walking was easier now and I half ran along the trail until I reached a knoll that overlooked the farmhouse and hid the farm in its own tidy valley. The house was draped with the fresh snow and reflected the yellow light emanating from within. It was a beautiful Christmas ornament, more beautiful than I had ever remembered.

The knoll was familiar to me. On summer evenings, as a child, I would sneak out of the house and climb the knoll to gaze at stars. I learned that darkness can be a friend. I learned that the night can conceal but it can also reveal for those willing to look and listen. It was a lesson I had forgotten.

Looking down from that knoll I felt the farmhouse's promise of warmth, the type of warmth that could only be found at the fireplace surrounded by family. That was when I realized I was home.

For years I had tried to make a home among the busy people in Chicago. But as hard as I tried, Chicago was only the place where I lived. This farmhouse, and the people inside, were home. As much as I wanted to be a big city hot shot, this was home and I was to be there for Christmas.

A few hundred yards and my journey would be complete. I leaned forward and sprinted toward the farmhouse. A ditch surprised me and I fell into a drift, but it was fun again. I was only a few steps from warmth and the snow against my face cheered me and strengthened my resolve. The aroma of burning wood from the fireplace tantalized my nostrils. I jumped to my feet and dashed to the house.

The snow cushioned my footsteps as I stood at the door. For a few seconds I gathered myself again and listened to muffled conversation inside. I choked back pressure in my throat and swallowed hard as I turned the door knob.

"Merry Christmas!" I shouted as I burst through the door. The family, even the little ones, were gathered around the fireplace until they saw I had arrived. There was sudden springing to feet, jumping and shouting.

Mother sat in her chair near the fire and fought back tears that soon won. Pop and the little ones were immediately upon me; it was a a pleasant mugging.

"I thought you wouldn't try to make it through the storm," Pop said. "It's really nasty out there."

"Yeah, but it's Christmas Eve and . . . you know . . . no one misses Christmas with the family."

The little ones helped me with my coat and I sat near the fire where Mother composed herself, and tried to hide the tears of a few moments earlier.

"It's nice to have the family together again." Her voice cracked but she fought it off. "How long can you stay, Nick?"

A few hours ago I planned to stay only long enough to be polite and complete "obligations." But the walk through the forest, the Indian, the cold, and memories changed my mind.

"At least a week."

"I didn't hear your car drive in." Mother was getting older but her ears were sharp as ever.

"No. It's down the road about two miles."

"You walked all that way?" Pop sounded like he didn't believe it. He glanced at my dress slacks and leather shoes and raised his eyebrows.

At the same time he took my light overcoat and walked toward an overloaded rack in a corner near the door. "Hey, this smells like smoke!"

"Yeah. Well, I took a shortcut through the woods. I almost froze except for the Indian along the way. . ."

"Indian?" Pop sounded even more incredulous.

"Yeah. There was an Indian with a fire in the woods. If it hadn't been for him, I might not have made it. I was in pretty bad shape for a while."

"Indian?" Pop raised his voice a little indicating his disbelief.

"Well, I was just about frozen, I could hardly walk and all, when I came across this Indian in the forest with a fire."

"A fire?"

"Yeah. He had a fire. I got warmed up then made it here. If he hadn't been there. . ."

"We'll talk about it later." Pop's face was flushed and skeptical and he hushed my protests as he ushered me into the kitchen with the coat in hand. "Don't spoil Christmas Eve with this kind of talk. You know there aren't any Indians around here. Have you been hitting the Christmas spirits?"

"No. Not at all. There really was this Indian. He had a black fur around him and a leather pouch, and a fire, and . . . well, smell my coat. It should still smell like the fire. That's how I found him. I smelled his fire."

Mother and the others knew something was going on and were a little uneasy. Pop sniffed the coat again and looked up with wide eyes. Then he took a good long smell of the fabric.

"We'd better call Bert about this," Pop finally decided with an air of certainty.

Bert Fairfield was an Indian expert. He knew a little about just about everything. He didn't display or use his knowledge in an arrogant way, but in a pleasant manner. He would share little bits of history and nostalgia that kept a conversation interesting.

Bert was most knowledgeable about Indians, though. He was part Indian himself. He had spent many hours in the library and talking to people to learn about local Indians. He had a filing system that rivalled the Smithsonian Institute and as much information as the Library of Congress. Bert made local Indians his hobby and his life. He was an undisputed expert, at least in the county

Pop grabbed the telephone and dialed Bert's number from memory. Bert would be busy with his family and Christmas celebrations of their own, but he was an old friend who lived on the county road. Most of all, he was accustomed to Pop's impulsiveness. Bert enjoyed adventure anyway, Christmas Eve or not.

"Yeah. Bert? Yeah. This is Jim. How are ya? Yeah. Merry Christmas, ho ho ho." Pop was stalling. He was a little apprehensive about explaining my evening trek to Bert.

"I'll tell you why I called, Bert. Sorry to bother you on Christmas Eve and all, but I need an expert opinion." Pop shifted his weight on his legs and began looking around. "Here, better yet, I'll let Nick explain what he saw. Yeah, he got in just a few minutes ago. Here, let him explain."

Pop took the easy way out. I didn't mind, though. I was as much interested in Bert's opinion as Pop was. I told Bert about getting stuck and trying to make it across the forest to the farm. I told him about the deer trail and about getting really cold. He said I was lucky I didn't die from exposure. He also had read about how some deer hunters die every year from exposure.

I told Bert about smelling the fire and nearly falling at the feet of the mysterious old Indian with the black fur around him. And I told Bert about how neither of us spoke.

Bert listened with a few "uh-huhs." He didn't ask about anything but the Indian's appearance. He was especially interested in that. I told him about his white hair, wrinkled face, leather pouch, and eyes that seemed to look both inside and beyond me.

He responded with another "uh-huh" and a long pause. I wondered what he was thinking. It wouldn't have been a surprise if he thought I was hallucinating from the cold. Pop sensed the pause and grabbed the phone.

"His coat smells like a fire, Bert. I didn't believe it myself. He didn't have any matches and his coat smells like a fire. I thought the Indians were long gone, Bert."

Pop responded to Bert with a few "uh-huhs" of his own, then hung up. "Bert said not to presume anything. We'll check it out tomorrow morning. Tonight, let's just forget about it and have a good time. It's Christmas. Right?"

"Right!" I was ready to forget the whole incident for the moment. Tension was building in Mother's face and her eyes followed us as we returned to the family room.

Pop explained to everyone that I had met someone out in the forest on my way and they were going to find him in the morning. Everyone seemed more at ease with that explanation but I could tell that Mother was going to find out a lot more that night. She wouldn't let Pop get a good night's sleep until he told her everything in detail—at least once.

Christmas Eve was as enjoyable and beautiful as ever. No. Really it was more beautiful. I had come home and understood what "home" really meant. Somewhere in that cold forest I had discovered a missing part of myself. Finally, home felt just right, not just for Christmas Eve, but for all time.

The little ones kept everyone's minds off the Indian and the confusion the forest adventure caused. The holiday evening made me even more grateful for his fire and the warmth it had given me. When everyone had eaten and drank as much as they could, told old stories, and laughed again and again, we went to the bedrooms that had been kept as though we had left them for only a minute. The old farmhouse was large enough to afford the space and the remembrance of the cold weather and deep snow outside made it cozier than I could ever recall.

It was quite early when I recognized the sunlight in the windows as the light of Christmas Day. I laid there for several minutes before I worked up enough energy to make my way downstairs. Already there was a commotion in the kitchen and when I had pulled my clothes on and made my way down, I found Bert was already there, sipping a cup of coffee.

Mother, Pop, and Bert were the only ones up. My brother and sisters' families were notoriously late risers and would probably sleep for a while yet, even on Christmas morning. Still, there was a quiet excitement as Bert and Pop went over what I had told them the previous evening.

"Ready to go?" I was barely awake and a known slow morning mover, but I like to sound perky even if I couldn't act the part. A few cups of coffee and I could handle the thought of bundling up and retrieving the car.

"Yeah. Let's go!" Bert sounded like he was ready for anything but he knew I was bluffing. I was surprised to see him so early. I

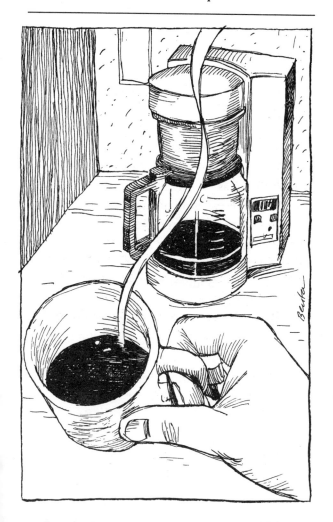

looked out the window and saw his snowmobile parked in the front yard. "Saw your car on the gravel road. Looks like you did a pretty good job of getting it stuck last night."

"Yeah. Once I was stuck I knew it. Do you think Johnny Pop will pull her out?"

"Oh, yeah!" Pop nearly jumped in his seat. He had such faith in that old friend of his. He would be just as confident if he were asked to use it to pull the Statue of Liberty to Detroit. As far as he was concerned, there wasn't anything that his old tractor couldn't do. I knew when I asked that I was just giving him a chance to brag about his old pal.

I drank my first cup of coffee quickly. I wanted to be as awake as I could before Bert started. He said he had been up until late looking up information on some of the local Indians. I had just dumped a teaspoon of sugar in my second cup when he started.

"I did some checking last night. I got out all my files on the Chippewas. They were the

Indians last in these parts. They got moved onto a no-good reservation up north. Some didn't go and took jobs on farms but for the most part they left. That was in the 1880s. There haven't been any real Chippewas in these parts since I can remember."

Bert leaned forward in his chair and cradled his coffee cup in tired hands. He peered into the cup as though he were reading what he wanted to say next.

"The Chippewas had some interesting legends, though. There was a great band of Indians that settled in this area a thousand years before the Chippewas. They were mostly primitives stuck in the Stone Age. They left mounds where they buried their dead. The Chippewas called them 'Ancients.'"

"They never saw them, though. The Ancients had died out for some reason. Disease maybe. The Chippewas, they were good on legends. They knew that the Ancients had been there before them."

Bert's voice trailed off as he talked. He set his coffee on the table and leaned back in his chair. Bert rubbed his hands together as he paused to collect his thoughts.

"I found one legend that tells how a medicine man of the Ancients went to seek a cure for an illness that had claimed many of his people. The medicine man searched for many days to find an herb that would end the fatal sickness. When he returned with the medicine, however, he found he was too late. His entire tribe had perished. The legend says the medicine man still wanders the land of his people looking for survivors of the great sickness."

Bert leaned forward again and rested his elbows on his legs and his head in his hands. He looked down at his feet where he moved his toes inside his shoes. Pop and Mother hadn't said a word but looked at each other several times as Bert reluctantly related his findings.

"You mean . . ." Dad started, but he couldn't finish before Bert broke in.

"I know it sounds far fetched, Jim. But there aren't any Indians around here and there haven't been for years and years. Even if there were, what would they be doing out on a night like last night?"

Bert's voice grew stronger as he tried to convince Pop.

"I followed Nick's tracks with the snowmobile when I came over." Bert's voice fell again and Mother and Pop listened and hung on his next words.

"Nick was in serious trouble last night. I found where you fell, Nick. Considering the wind and temperature, there is no way he could have made it unless he was dressed much warmer than he was. The snow had just about covered the tracks until a place on the ridge."

Bert spoke slowly to choose his words carefully.

"There was a place where Nick stopped and knelt down. The tracks became clear after that all the way to the house. There must have been something there last night that isn't there now. By all rights, Nick should have died in that forest last night."

"No ashes? No other tracks? No burnt wood?" Pop was looking for some hard evidence.

"No. Nothing. No sign of anything except Nick's tracks," Bert's voice was clear. He had made his point and neither Mother nor Pop were going to question his credibility.

"You should know that the Indian culture is based on these types of legends. I'm not going to try and explain it or make any sense out of it. I just wanted you to know what I found. You decide what you want to. I just know Nick wouldn't have made it without something there. That's all."

Bert was uncomfortable defending his legend explanation but he wasn't about to pass it off, either. "Don't presume anything, Jim. Especially on Christmas. Maybe we should leave it at that."

I, too, was ready to leave it at that. The old Indian was gone, the fire seemed to have never existed, and I had made an impossible journey in the middle of a dangerous blizzard without harm. "Yes," I thought, "it is best to leave it at that."

"Maybe you're right." Pop's voice was low and trailed off as though he was still in thought. "Let's see if Johnny Pop will pull that car out of the ditch. We'll have the presents under the tree before the others are awake."

Pop, Bert, and I bundled up and went to the barn. Mother began preparing another mountain of food.

The fresh white snow sparkled in the morning sun. Johnny Pop started on the third crank. Its two-cylinder rhythm was a familiar sound that could be heard for miles.

As it turned out, I stayed home for two weeks that Christmas. That spring, I bundled up my best adjectives and moved into a small home not far from Walker's Hill. Life is good.

Of course, life isn't perfect in Duncan, but I don't think life was ever intended to be easy all the time. But when I find myself sitting alone late at night wondering about decisions made long ago, I am comforted. Very often, like some distant voice in the wilderness, the unmistakeable aroma of a campfire comes to me like an old friend. Then, all doubts disappear.

I am not prone to believing in ghosts or spirits or things that go bump in the night. But I know something remarkable, something. . . perhaps a miracle, happened that Christmas Eve in the woods. And if a miracle can happen on Christmas Eve, why not other days?

Yes, Christmas is not just for children. Perhaps it is especially for those of us who have lost ourselves along the way.

Merry Christmas.